WHO GOT RID OF ANGUS FLINT?

How do you get rid of a guest who picks you up by the hair, won't let you play the piano, watch television or shut the window? Candida and her family try everything – they poison his stew and litter the house with roller-skates in the hope that he will fall over them – but nothing makes him leave . . .

WHO GOT RID OF ANGUS FLINT?

DIANA WYNNE JONES

Illustrated by John Sewell

A Magnet Book

First published in this form 1978
by Evans Brothers Limited
Magnet edition first published 1980
by Methuen Children's Books Ltd
11 New Fetter Lane, London EC4P 4EE

Text copyright © 1975 Diana Wynne Jones
Illustrations copyright © 1978 Evans Brothers Limited
Printed in Great Britain by
Richard Clay (The Chaucer Press), Ltd.,
Bungay, Suffolk

ISBN 0 416 88480 6

Contents

Angus Flint
Arrives

The day my sister Cora went away for a fortnight, a friend of Dad's called Angus Flint rang
up out of the blue. He said his wife had just left
him, so could he come and see us to cheer himself up? I don't know how my father came to
have a friend like Angus Flint. They met at
college. One of them must have been different.

Candida Robbins is an Awful
Girl.   official!
            signed Pip.

Trust my awful little brother to ruin this paper, when Angus Flint stole all the rest. Pip's never recovered from Cora once rashly telling him he was a genius, and he thinks *he* was the one who got rid of Angus Flint. And I'm not awful. Things just happen to me.

Anyway, Dad was pleased Angus Flint had not forgotten him, so he said "Yes," and then told Mum. Mum said "Oh," in the blank sort of way I do when I find my brothers have pinched all my chocolate. Then she said, "I suppose he can have Cora's room." Imagine the way an Ancient Roman might say, "I suppose the lions can have my best friend," and you'll know how she said it.

That ought to have been a warning because Mum can like people no sane person can stand, but I was doing my piano practice, so I didn't attend. Miss Hawksmoore had given me an all-time big hit to work on called *Elfin Dance*, and I was grinding my teeth at it. It sounds like two very glum medium-sized elephants trying to waltz. And the next number in my book is a top pop called *Fairy Rondeau*. I only carry on because I like our piano so much. It's a great, black, grand piano that Mum bought for £10, cheap at £1000 to our minds.

Pip can't decide what he's a genius *at*, but, a little while ago, he thought he might be a genius at playing the piano. He was doing his practice when Angus Flint arrived. But before that, Pip and Tony—Tony's the brother between me and Pip—had been so glad that Cora was not around to henpeck them that they had celebrated by eating—Well, they wouldn't say what they had eaten, but Tony had come out in spots and been sick. Tony has the art of looking bland and vague when any misdeed happens. Mum thought he really was ill. When Angus Flint breezed in, Tony was in a chair in the sitting-room with a bowl on his knees, and Mum was fussing.

Now this shows you what Angus Flint was like. Mum went to shake hands, saying she was sorry we were at sixes and sevens. And she explained that Tony had been taken ill.

Angus Flint said, "Then open the window. I don't want to get it." Those were his first words. He was square and stumpy, and he had a blank sort of face with a pout to it. His voice was loud and jolly.

Mum looked rather taken aback, but she slid the big window open a little and told Tony to go to bed. Dad asked Angus Flint to sit down. Angus Flint looked critically at the chairs and then sat in the best one. Dad had just begun to ask him where he was living these days, when he bounced up again.

"This is a horribly uncomfortable chair. It's not fit to sit in," he said.

We hadn't done anything to it—though I wish we had now—it was just that the chair is one of Mum's bargains. All our furniture is bargains. But Pip looked at me meaningly and grinned, because I was shuddering. I can't bear anyone to insult a piece of furniture to its face. No matter how ugly or uncomfortable a chair or a table is, I don't think it should be told. It can't help it, poor thing. I know most of our furniture is hideous, and most of the chairs hurt you sooner or later, but there's no need to say so. But I don't think furniture can read, so I don't mind writing it.

Meanwhile, Dad got out of the chair Tony had been sitting in and suggested Angus Flint sat there. "Not that one," Angus Flint said. "That's infested with germs." He ignored all the other chairs and marched over to mine. "I want to sit down," he told me.

"Let Angus have your chair, Candida," Mum said.

I was furious, but I got up. People seem to think children have no rights. Pip made his Dying Chinaman face at me out of sympathy. Then he spun round on the piano-stool, put his foot down on the loud pedal and slammed into *How Shall I Thy True-love Know?* He's only got

as far as that one. Tony says he'd know Pip's True-love anywhere: she's tone-deaf, with a stutter. She sounds worse with the loud pedal down.

Angus Flint was explaining in his loud jolly voice that he'd taken up Yoga since his wife left him. "You should all do Yoga," he said. "It's very profound. It—" He stopped. Pip's True-love did a booming stutter and made a wrong note. Angus Flint roared, "Stop fooling with that piano, can't you! I'm talking."

"I've got to practise," Pip said.

"Not while I'm here," said Angus Flint. Then, before I could do anything, he sprang up and lifted Pip off the piano-stool by his hair. It hurt Pip a lot—as I found out later for myself—but Pip managed to walk out of the room and not even look as if he were crying. My parents were stunned. They are just far too polite to guests. But I'm not.

"Do that again," I said, "and I shall personally see that you suffer."

All I got from Angus Flint was a blank angry stare, and he went back to my chair. "This is a stupid chair," he said. "It's far too low." The Stare turned out to be his great weapon. He used it on anything he disliked. I kept getting it. Mostly, it was over shutting the window. It's such a big window that, when it's

open, it's like having half the sitting-room wall missing. I got colder and colder. I thought Tony's imaginary germs must have gone by now, so I got up and shut it.

Angus Flint did not stop his loud jolly talk to Dad. He just got up and opened it again, talking all the time. I wasn't having that, so I got up and shut it. Angus Flint got up and opened it. I forget how many times we did this. In between, Angus Flint patted Menace. At least—I think he thought he was patting Menace, but Menace had every excuse to think he was being beaten.

"Good little dog, this," Angus Flint kept saying. Clout, thump!

"Don't hit him so hard," I said. I got the Stare again, so I got up and shut the window. While Angus Flint was opening it, Menace saved his ribs from being broken by squeezing under one of the cupboards and staying there. The space was small even for a dachshund.

The Smell
in the Night

Menace didn't even come out from under the
cupboard for supper, although it smelt delicious.
Mum puts forth her best for visitors. Serve
Tony right. He didn't want any.

If you pinch my paper

you not to insult me on it.

signed, Tony Robbins.

OK, OK. Mum's turn to be insulted.
Angus Flint cut off a very small corner of his
veal and nibbled at it like a rabbit. "This
is nice, Margaret!" he said. He sounded
thoroughly surprised, as if Mum was famous
for cooking fried toads in snail sauce. Then he
went on telling Dad that the Common Market
was very profound. Mum was looking stormy
and Dad seemed crushed by then. So I told
Angus Flint that it wasn't profound at all. I
didn't see why I shouldn't. After all, I am going
to have the vote one day. But I got the Stare
Treatment again, and then Angus Flint said,
"I don't want to listen to childish nonsense."
   I felt almost crushed too. I was glad it was
Pass the Buck, Dad on the telly. Pip and I did the
washing up in order to see it, and Tony got out
of bed—he'd watch that programme if he was
dying. We were all crouched around the television, ready to go, when Angus Flint came

bustling in from the sitting-room where Mum was giving him polite coffee, and turned it over to the other channel. We all yelled at him.

"But you must watch *Battered Brides*," he said. "It's very profound."

Profound my left fibula! It's one of those awful series about girls sharing a flat. They undress a lot, which accounts for Angus Flint finding it profound. And he stood over the knob, too, so we couldn't turn it back without wrecking the telly. Tony was so furious that he stormed off to fetch Dad, and Pip and I raced after him.

Dad said, "I've had about enough of Angus!" which is strong language from him, and Mum said, "So have I!" and we all thundered back to the dining-room.

And, would you believe this? Angus Flint was standing on his head, doing Yoga, watching *Battered Brides* upside-down! You can't argue with someone who's upside-down. We tried, but it just can't be done. Instead of a face, you have to talk to a pair of maroon socks—with a hole in one toe—nodding gently at eye-level. The face you ought to be arguing with is on the floor, squashed and purple-looking and the wrong way up. And when you've talked to the socks for a while, the squashed face on the floor says, "I have to stay like this for ten more

minutes," and you give up and go away. You have to.

We went to bed. I don't know how my parents managed for the rest of the evening, but I can guess. I heard them coming to bed. Dad was most earnestly probing to find out when Angus Flint intended to go. From the strong silence that followed, I gathered that Dad was getting the Stare Treatment too.

In the middle of the night, we were all woken up by a dreadful smell of burning. We thought the house was on fire at first. We were quite pleased, because that's one thing that's never happened to us yet. But the smell turned out to come from the kitchen. It was thick and black, like when you burn toffee.

So we all rushed to the kitchen. Angus Flint was there, calmly stuffing what looked like clean white sheets into the boiler.

"I had to burn these," he said. "They were covered with sugar or something."

"I could have washed them," said Mum.

She got the Stare. "They were ruined," said Angus Flint.

I looked at Pip. He was horribly disappointed. He had always had such faith in sugar for beds. It's supposed to melt and make the victim sticky as well as scratchy. I've told him over and over again that it's worth taking the time to catch fleas off Menace. But I suppose Angus Flint would have burnt the sheets for fleas too.

He went to bed with clean sheets—Mum made his bed, because he never then, or any other time, did a thing himself—saying he would sleep late next morning. In fact, he got up before I did and ate my breakfast. Dad fled then. He said he had an urgent experiment at the lab. The coward. He saw me coming. And I couldn't complain to Mum either, because Angus Flint took her over and told her all morning how his wife had left him.

We heard quite a lot of it. The story had a sort of chorus which went, "Well, I couldn't stand for that, and I had to hit her." The chorus came so many times that the poor woman must have been black and blue. No wonder she left him! If I were her, I would have—Well, perhaps not, because, as we were swiftly finding out, Angus Flint was quite immune to anything ordinary people could do.

Mum was tired out by lunch-time. "Get lunch, Candida," she said. "I'm going out. I've got the—er—a meeting. I shan't be in till nearly seven."

That was how our heartless and cowardly parents left Tony, Pip and me alone all and every day with Angus Flint.

Roller-skates
and Stew

Of course we objected to being left alone with
Angus Flint. Dad said that it was fair shares,
because they had him all evening. My mother
had the cheek to say to us, "Well, darlings, if

you three can't get rid of him, nobody can."

I raved at her. She didn't know what it was like. He took Pip's football away because he said we were making a noise with it. He took all the mouth-organs, and Tony's trains. Tony has a way of leaving half-made models about, and Angus Flint used to take them apart whenever he came across them. He said they were in the way. When I went to complain, he was standing on his head.

He always stood on his head after he'd done anything like that. He stood on his head after he stole my paper. All I'd done was to make a bad drawing of Angus Flint standing on his head. He'd no business to look at my private paper anyway. I drew it because I was so mad at the way Angus Flint would keep insulting the furniture. The boys can stick up for themselves, but Cora's bed can't. Angus Flint said it was lumpy and hard. He told the dining-table it was rickety and the chairs they were only fit for scrap. He said the sitting-room furniture ought to be burnt.

Tony said that if he hated our furniture so much, he should leave. He got the Stare. Pip asked Angus Flint every day when he was going, but he only got the Stare too. I knew it was no good telling Angus Flint to stop insulting the furniture, so, whenever he complained,

I said, "That's a very profound idea." And got the Stare.

After that, the boys went round calling everything "Very profound," from the curtains to our comics. Angus Flint must have felt they had something. All our comics suddenly disappeared. After searching everywhere else, we found them in Cora's room, where Angus Flint had been reading them. I rushed at Angus Flint to complain, and there he was, standing on his head again, maroon socks waving, and his face, squashed and purple, giving me the Stare upside-down at floor-level.

"Go away. I've got to do this for five more minutes."

"It looks very profound," I said, but I went away quickly while I was saying it. By that time, I was scared of being picked up by my hair again.

I got picked up by my hair for rescuing Menace. Menace did not appear very often for fear of being patted by Angus Flint. He lurked nervously under cupboards. But one morning he rashly lay down outside the boys' room. Pip and Tony decided that Menace would be able to slide into hiding more easily if he had one of my old roller-skates strapped to his middle.

Menace hated the idea.

I heard him hating it and came to help.

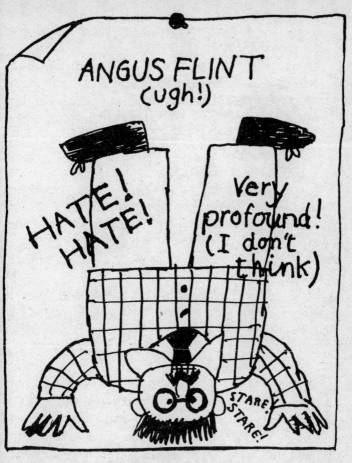

There was a lot of shouting, and a good deal more yelping from Menace. Then Angus Flint came pelting out of Cora's room roaring at us to be quiet.

Menace fled. He never let Angus Flint get within a foot of him if he could help it. But the skate stayed. Angus Flint trod on it and shot off downstairs. It was beautiful. We were all sorry when he stopped on the first landing. Then he came pounding upstairs again shouting, "Whose skate was that?"

I said, "Mine," without thinking.

I was picked up and swung about by my hair. It must have hurt me more than Pip, because I'm heavier.

Still, that put an idea into my sore head. I went and borrowed roller-skates from everyone I knew. I got armfuls. Pip and Tony helped me bring them home in carrier bags. There we laid them out, like you do mousepoison, in cunning corners. It was an awful nuisance. Kids kept coming to the door saying, "My sister says she lent you my roller-skates, and she's no right to do that because they're mine." But there were quite a few left, even after that.

The result: Pip fell over once, Tony twice, and me three times. Mum and Dad were immune. They said they'd had years of practice. And Angus Flint never said whether he'd fallen over or not. He simply collected all the skates up and threw them in the dust-bin. He did it just before the dust-men called, so they were gone before we realized. And kids still keep coming to the door to ask for their skates. I've had to part with most of my nicest things in return.

Tony got picked up by his hair because of the plastic stew. He wanted revenge because Angus Flint kept breaking his models. And Tony hated the way Angus Flint always took one rabbit nibble at his food and then sounded so surprised that it was nice. Tony got as annoyed over that as I did at the way Angus Flint kept insulting the furniture. Mum was furious too. After the third time Angus Flint did it, she took to saying pleasantly, "Arsenic does taste nice." At which Angus Flint always gave the same loud jolly laugh. So I think Mum and Tony put their heads together over the stew.

No we didn't.

Mum just pretended not to see.

Tony.

I'm writing this, not you, Tony Robbins. And you said I could have your paper.

As I was saying, it was stew for supper. Tony had collected all the bits of left-over plastic model he could find. You know the things you have left after you've made a model. They look like knobby fishbones. Tony had collected them from everywhere he could think of. Because most of them came from the floor or the backs of cupboards, there was a good deal of grit and fluff and Menace's hairs with them too. Mum put the first spoonful of stew on Angus Flint's plate, and while she was dipping for the second spoonful, Tony dumped a great handful of mixed plastic and fluff on top of it. Mum never turned a hair. She just poured orange gravy over the lot and passed it to Angus Flint.

We all watched breathlessly while he took up a forkful and did his nibble. "This—" he began as usual. Then he found what it was. He spat it out. "Who did this?" he said. He knew it was Tony by instinct. He answered his own question by picking Tony up by his hair and carrying him out of the room.

Mum knocked over her chair and rushed out after them. But by the time we all got to the hall—we got in one another's way a little—Tony was upstairs running his head under the cold tap. And Angus Flint was—Yes, you guessed it!—upside-down on the hall carpet.

"I don't want any supper, Margaret," his squashed face said.

Mum said "Good!" to the maroon socks and stormed back to the dining-room.

Cream Teas

Next morning, there was nothing for breakfast. Angus Flint had got up in the night and eaten all the cornflakes and all the milk, and fried himself all the eggs.

"Why is there no food?" he demanded.

"You ate it all," Mum said.

Angus Flint did not seem to notice how cold she sounded. He just set to work to eat all the bread and marmalade too. He simply did not see how we all hated him. He really enjoyed staying with us. He kept saying so. Every evening when my parents crawled home to him, he would meet them with a beaming smile. "This is such a friendly household, Margaret," he said. "You've done me a lot of good."

"I think we must be very profound," Pip said drearily.

"I suppose I couldn't live here always?" said Angus Flint.

There was silence. A very profound one.

Pip broke the silence by stumping off to do his practice. By that time, the only time either of us dared practise was when our parents were at home. Angus Flint would not let us touch the piano. If you started, he came and picked you up by your hair. Pip and I got so that we used to dive off the stool and under the piano as soon as we heard a footstep. Pip's True-love, when he did manage to play her, seemed to have developed a squint as well as a stutter, and as for my gloomy elephants, they had got more like despairing dinosaurs. I kept having to apologize to the piano—not to speak of Miss Hawksmoore.

"You should sell that piano," Angus Flint said, as Pip started bashing away.

Mum would not hear of it. The piano is her best bargain ever. Not everyone can buy a perfect concert-grand for £10. Besides, she wanted us to learn to play it.

By this time, Angus Flint had stayed with us for nearly a fortnight. Cora was due home in three days, and he still showed no signs of leaving. The boys told him he would have to leave when Cora came back, but all they got was the Stare. My parents both realized that something would have to be done and began to show a little firmness at last. Mum explained— in her special anxious way that she uses when she doesn't want to offend someone—that Cora was coming back soon and would need her room. Dad took to starting everything he said to Angus Flint with "When you leave us—" But Angus Flint took not the slightest bit of notice. It began to dawn on me that he really did intend to stay for good.

I was soon sure of it. He suddenly went all charming. He left me some breakfast for once. He even made his bed, and he was polite all morning. I warned the boys, but they wouldn't believe me. I warned Mum too, when she came

back suddenly in the middle of the afternoon, but it was a hot day and she was too tired to listen.

"I only keep buying things if I stay out," she said. "I'd rather face Angus Flint than the Bank Manager."

Too right she kept buying things. That week, she'd bought two hideous three-legged tables for the sitting-room, about eight bookcases, and four rolled-up carpets. We were beginning to look like an old furniture store.

Angus Flint heard Mum come back. He rushed up to her with a jolly smile on his face. "Isn't it a lovely day, Margaret? What do you say to me taking you and the kids out to tea somewhere?"

Mum agreed like a shot. He hadn't paid for a thing up to then. The boys had visions of ice-cream and cream buns. I knew there was a catch in it, but it was just the day for tea out on a lawn somewhere, and I did feel we ought at least to get that out of Angus Flint in return for all our suffering. So we all crammed into his car.

Angus Flint drove exactly like you might expect, far too fast. He honked his horn a lot, overtook everything he could—particularly on corners—and he expected old ladies to leap like deer in order not to be run over. Mum said what about the Copper Kettle? Tony said the cakes in the other place were better. But Angus Flint insisted that he had seen "A perfect little place," on his way to stay with us.

We drove three times round town looking for the perfect little place, at top speed. Our name was mud in every street by then. We called out whenever we saw a cafe of any kind after a while, but Angus Flint just said, "We can't stop here," and sped on.

After nearly an hour, when Pip was near despair, we ended up roaring through Palham, which is a village about three miles out of town. There was a Tea Shoppe with striped umbrellas. Our spirit was broken by then. We didn't even mention it. But Angus Flint stopped with a screech of brakes. "This looks as if it might do," he said.

We all piled out and sat under an umbrella.

"Well, what will you have?" said Angus Flint.

Deep breaths were drawn and cream teas for five were ordered. We all waited, looking forward to cream and cakes. We felt we really deserved our teas.

Angus Flint said, "I've applied for a job in your town, Margaret. The interview's tomorrow. Your husband was good enough to say that I could make my home with you. Don't you think that's a good idea?"

We stared. Had Dad said that?

"There's Cora," Mum said. "We've no room."

"That's no problem," Angus Flint said. "You can put the two girls in together."

"No!" I said. If you knew Cora—!

"I'd pay," Angus Flint said, joking and trying to be nice. "A nominal sum—a pound a month, say?"

Mum drew herself up resolutely, to my great relief. "No, Angus. It's absolutely out of the question. You'll have to go as soon as Cora comes back."

Angus Flint did not answer. Instead, he bounced jovially to his feet. "I have to go and see someone for a moment," he said. "I shan't be long. Don't wait for me." And he was back in his car and driving away before any of us could move.

Angus Flint's Revenge

They brought us five cream teas almost at once. It was a perfect revenge.

Mum could not believe that Angus Flint was not coming back. We ate our cream teas.

After a while, Mum let the boys eat Angus's cream tea too, and said we could order another when he came back. When they came with the bill, she said we were expecting a friend, who would pay.

Half an hour later, they began to look at us oddly.

Half an hour after that, they took the umbrellas out of the tables and stood the chairs on them suggestively.

A short while after that, they came and asked to be paid. They made it quite clear that they knew we were trying to cheat them. They refused Mum's desperately offered cheque. We had to go through all our pockets and shake Mum's bag out on the table, and even then we were 2p short. They forgave us that, but grimly. They looked after us unlovingly as we went. Mum nearly sank under the embarrassment.

Then we had to walk home. It was still hot. Tony hates walking, and he whined. Pip got a blister and whined too. Mum snarled and I snapped. We were all in the worst tempers of our lives by the time we plunged up the garden path and burst into the house. We knew that Angus Flint would be standing there, upside-down on the hall carpet, to meet us.

"And this time I shan't care that it's his socks I'm talking to!" I said.

But the person standing in the hall was Dad. He was the right way up, of course, and wondering where we'd all got to. Mum went for him with both fangs out. "Have you had the nerve to tell Angus Flint that he could live with us? If so—" I felt quite sorry for my father. He admitted that, in the heat of the first reunion, he might have said some such thing, but—Oh boy! Never have I heard my mother give tongue like she did then. I couldn't do it half so well. Even Cora couldn't, the time she acted King Herod at school.

After that, for a beautiful, peaceful half evening, we thought Angus Flint had gone for good. We kept the window shut, played the piano, watched the things we wanted on the telly, and cheered Dad up by playing cards with him. We were all thoroughly happy, when Angus Flint came back again. He knew we were likely to complain, I suppose, so he brought a girlfriend home with him to make sure we couldn't go for him.

The girlfriend was a complete stranger to us. Hand picked for idiocy, with glasses and a giggle.

"Teach her to play cards," said Angus Flint. "She's quite clever really."

She wasn't. But neither was Angus Flint, when it came to cards. Have you ever played

cards with somebody who thinks for twenty minutes before he puts a card down, and then puts down exactly the wrong one? He played the girl's hand too, though she was slightly better at it than he was. We went to bed after the first game. But Angus Flint didn't take the girlfriend home until well after midnight. I know, because I heard Mum let fly again when he did.

Angus Flint came back at three and woke me up hammering at the front door.

When I let him in, he said, "Didn't you hear me knocking? I might have caught my death."

I said, "I wish you had!" and escaped into the sitting-room before he could pick me up by my hair.

Menace was there. He crawled nervously out from under the piano to be stroked.

"Menace," I said. "Where's your spirit? Can't you bite Angus Flint?"

Then I thought that I didn't dare bite Angus Flint either, and got so miserable that I went wandering round the room. I patted the uncomfortable chairs and the poor ugly tables, and stroked the piano.

"Chairs," I said, "stand up for yourselves! He insults you all the time. Tables," I said, "he said you ought to be burnt! Piano, he told Mum to sell you. Do something, all of you! Furniture of the world, unite!" I made them a very stirring speech, all about the rights of oppressed furniture, and it made me feel much better. Not that I thought it would do any good. But I thought it was a very good idea.

She thinks it was her idea but I'd been doing that for a whole week then.
    signed PIP.
Me too, Tony.

The Tables Turn

Next morning, Angus Flint ate my breakfast as usual, and Mum and Dad went out together to make friends again. Leaving us alone with Angus Flint, yet again!

At least there was something "very pro-found" on the telly that afternoon. First I ever knew that racehorses were profound, but it meant twenty minutes' peace. I did some prac-tice. The piano sounded lovely. My elfin elephants shrank in size and were beginning to sound like mere hobnailed goblins, when the door was torn open. I knew it was Angus Flint and dived for safety.

He was in a very bad temper. I think his horse lost. As I crawled out from under the piano, he sat down at it, grumbling, and started to hammer out a sonata. I was surprised to see that he knew how to play. But he played very badly. Menace began to whine under his cupboard.

Angus Flint thumped both hands down with a jangle. "This is a horrible piano," he said. "It's got a terrible tone, and it needs tuning."

Rotten slander. I don't blame the piano for getting annoyed. Its curved black rear shuddered. One of its stumpy front legs pawed the ground. Then its lid shut with a clap on Angus Flint's fingers. Now I know why Mum got it for only £10. Angus Flint dragged his fingers free with such a yell that Pip and Tony came to see what was happening.

By the time they got there, both the new,

ugly little tables were stealing towards Angus Flint for a surprise attack, each with their three legs twinkling cautiously over the carpet. Angus Flint saw one out of the corner of his eye and turned to Stare at it. It stood where it was, looking innocent. But the piano-stool spun itself round and tipped him on the floor. I think that was very loyal of the stool, because it must have been the one piece of furniture Angus Flint had not insulted. And, while Angus

Flint was sprawling on the floor, the best chair trundled up and did its best to run him over. He scrambled out of its way with a howl. And the nearest bookcase promptly showered him with books. While he was trying to get up, the piano lowered its music-stand and charged.

I don't blame Angus Flint for being terrified. The piano was gnashing its keys at him and kicking out with its pedals and snorting through the holes in its music-stand. And it went galloping around the room after Angus Flint on its three brass castors like a mad, black bull. The rest of the furniture kept blundering across his path. Tables knocked him this way and that, and chairs herded him into huddles of other chairs. But they always left him a free way to run when the piano charged, so that he had a thoroughly frightening time. They never once tried to hurt the three of us.

I stuffed myself into a corner and admired. That piano was an expert. It would come thundering down on Angus Flint. When he tore off frantically sideways, it stopped short and banged its lid down within inches of his trouser-seat. It could turn in its own length and be after him again before you could believe it to be possible. Angus Flint dashed round and round the sitting-room, and the piano thundered after him, and when the boys had to leave

the doorway, one of the new bookcases dodged over and stood across it, so that Angus Flint was utterly trapped.

"Do something, can't you!" he kept howling at me, and I only laughed.

The reason the boys had to leave the doorway was that the dining-room table had heard the fun going on and wanted to join in. The trouble was, both its rickety wings were spread out and it was too wide to get through the dining-room door. It was in the doorway, clattering its feet and banging furiously for help. Tony and Pip took pity on it and took its wings down. It then scuttled across the hall, nudged aside the bookcase, and dived into the sitting-room after Angus Flint, flapping both wings like a great angry bird. And it wasn't going to play cat and mouse like the piano. It was out to get Angus Flint. He had some very narrow escapes and howled louder than ever.

I thought the time had come to widen the scene a little. I made my way around the walls, with tables and chairs trundling this way and that all around me, and opened the window.

Angus Flint howled out that I was a good girl—which annoyed me—and made for the opening like a bat out of hell. I meant to trip him when he got there. I didn't want him getting too much of a start. But the carpet saved me the trouble by flipping up one of its corners around his feet. He came down on his face, half inside the room and half in the garden. The piano and the dining-table both bore down on him. He scrambled up and bolted. I've never seen anyone run so fast.

The table was after him like a shot, but the piano got its rear castor stuck on the sill. It must be very awkward having to gallop with only

one leg at the back. I went to help it, but the faithful piano-stool and my favourite chair got there first and heaved it free. Then it hunched its wide front part and fairly shot across the garden and out into the road after the flying Angus Flint. The chairs and tables all set out too, bravely bobbling and trundling. Last of all went Menace, barking as if he was doing all the chasing single-handed.

I don't know what the other people in the street thought. The dining-table collided with a lamp-post half-way down the street and put itself out of the running. But the piano got up speed wonderfully and was hard on Angus Flint's heels as he shot into the next street. After that, we lost them. We were too busy collecting exhausted tables and chairs, which were strewn all down the street. The piano-stool had only got as far as the garden gate, and my favourite chair broke a castor getting through the window. We had to carry them back to the house. And there was a fair amount of tidying up to do indoors, what with the books, the carpets, and Cora's bed.

Cora's bed, probably the most insulted piece of furniture in the house, must have been frantic to get at Angus Flint too. It had forced itself half-way through the bedroom door and then stuck. We had a terrible job getting it back inside the room. We had just done it, and were wearily trying to mend the dining-table—which has never been the same since—when we heard twanging and clattering noises coming from the sitting-room. We were in time to see the piano come plodding back through the window and put itself in its usual place. It looked tired but satisfied.

"Do you think it's eaten him?" Pip said hopefully.

The piano didn't say. But it hadn't. Mum and Dad came back and we were all cheerfully having a cup of tea when Angus Flint suddenly came shooting downstairs. We think he climbed up the drainpipe in order not to meet the piano again. I suspect that Cora's bed was rather glad to see him.

"I'm just leaving," Angus Flint said.

It was music to our ears! He went straight out to his car too, carrying his suitcase. We all came out to say polite good-bye—or polite good-riddance, as Tony put it.

"I've had a wonderful time," Angus Flint said. "Here's a football for you, Pip." And he held out to Pip a flat orange thing. It was Pip's own football, but it was burst. "And this is for you," he said to Tony, handling him a fistful of broken plastic. Then he said to me, "I'm giving you some paper." And he gave me one sheet of

my own paper. One sheet! I'd had a whole new block.

"I do hope Cora's bed bit you," I said sweetly.

Angus Flint gave me the Stare for that, but it wasn't as convincing as usual, somehow. Then he got into his car and drove away. Actually drove away and didn't come back. We cheered.

It's been so peaceful since. Mum wondered whether to sell the new tables, but we wouldn't let her. They are our faithful friends. As for the piano, well, Pip has decided he's going to be a genius at something else instead. His excuse for giving up lessons is that Miss Hawksmoore's false teeth make her spit on his hands when she's teaching him. They do. But the real reason is that he's scared of the piano. I'm not. I love it more than that coward Menace even, and I'm determined to work and work until I've learnt how to play it as it deserves.

If you have enjoyed this book you might like
to read the other titles in the Jesters series

**The Spy and the Mission of Staggering
Importance
The Deadly Gang
The Terrible Kidnapping of Cyril Bonhamy**

More exciting titles will be following soon